The

Illustrated

Frankenstein

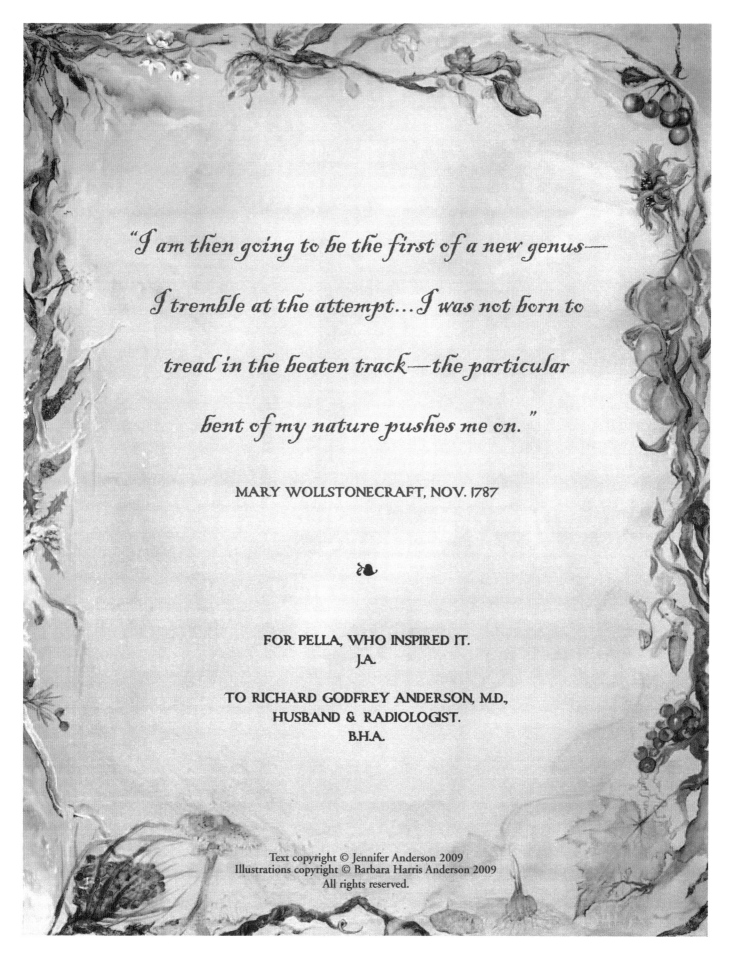

"I am then going to be the first of a new genus—
I tremble at the attempt…I was not born to
tread in the beaten track—the particular
bent of my nature pushes me on."

MARY WOLLSTONECRAFT, NOV. 1787

FOR PELLA, WHO INSPIRED IT.
J.A.

TO RICHARD GODFREY ANDERSON, M.D.,
HUSBAND & RADIOLOGIST.
B.H.A.

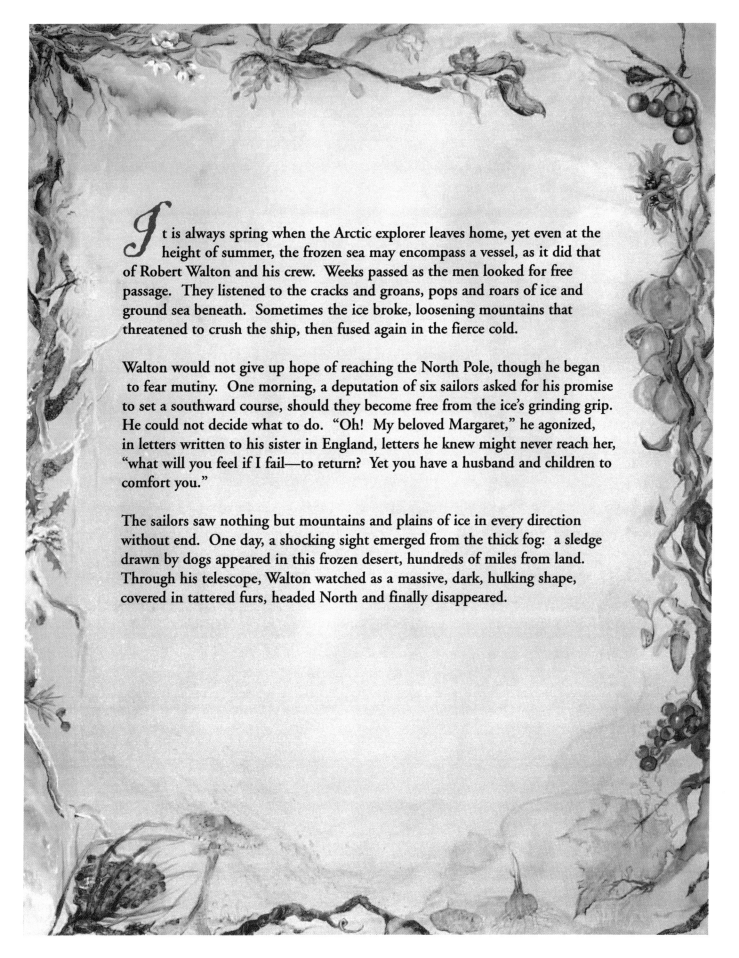

*I*t is always spring when the Arctic explorer leaves home, yet even at the height of summer, the frozen sea may encompass a vessel, as it did that of Robert Walton and his crew. Weeks passed as the men looked for free passage. They listened to the cracks and groans, pops and roars of ice and ground sea beneath. Sometimes the ice broke, loosening mountains that threatened to crush the ship, then fused again in the fierce cold.

Walton would not give up hope of reaching the North Pole, though he began to fear mutiny. One morning, a deputation of six sailors asked for his promise to set a southward course, should they become free from the ice's grinding grip. He could not decide what to do. "Oh! My beloved Margaret," he agonized, in letters written to his sister in England, letters he knew might never reach her, "what will you feel if I fail—to return? Yet you have a husband and children to comfort you."

The sailors saw nothing but mountains and plains of ice in every direction without end. One day, a shocking sight emerged from the thick fog: a sledge drawn by dogs appeared in this frozen desert, hundreds of miles from land. Through his telescope, Walton watched as a massive, dark, hulking shape, covered in tattered furs, headed North and finally disappeared.

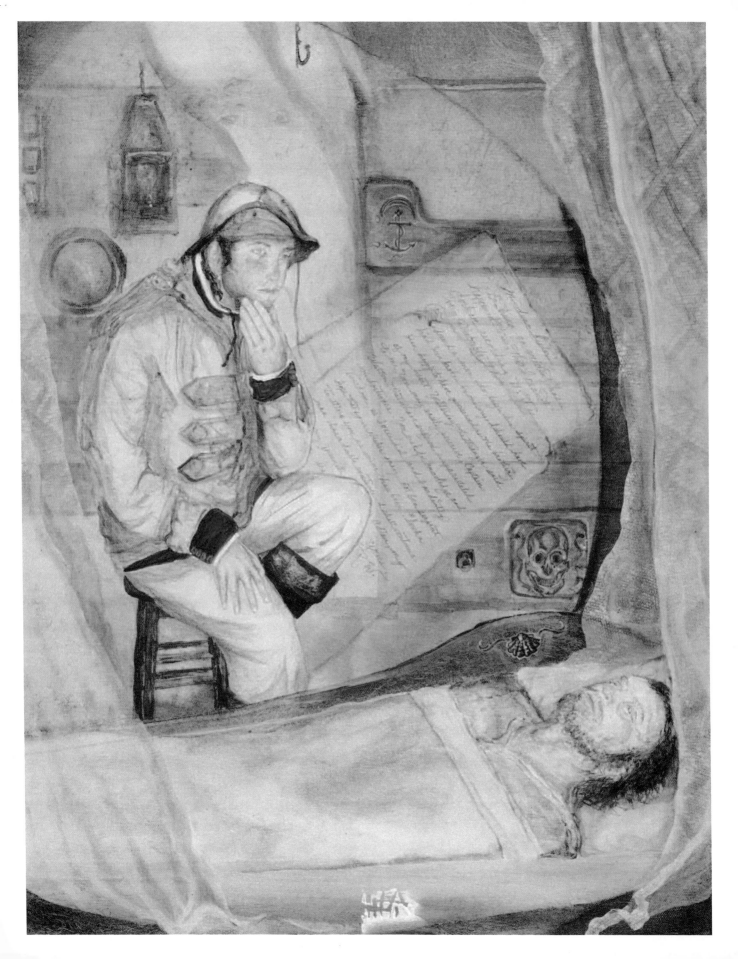

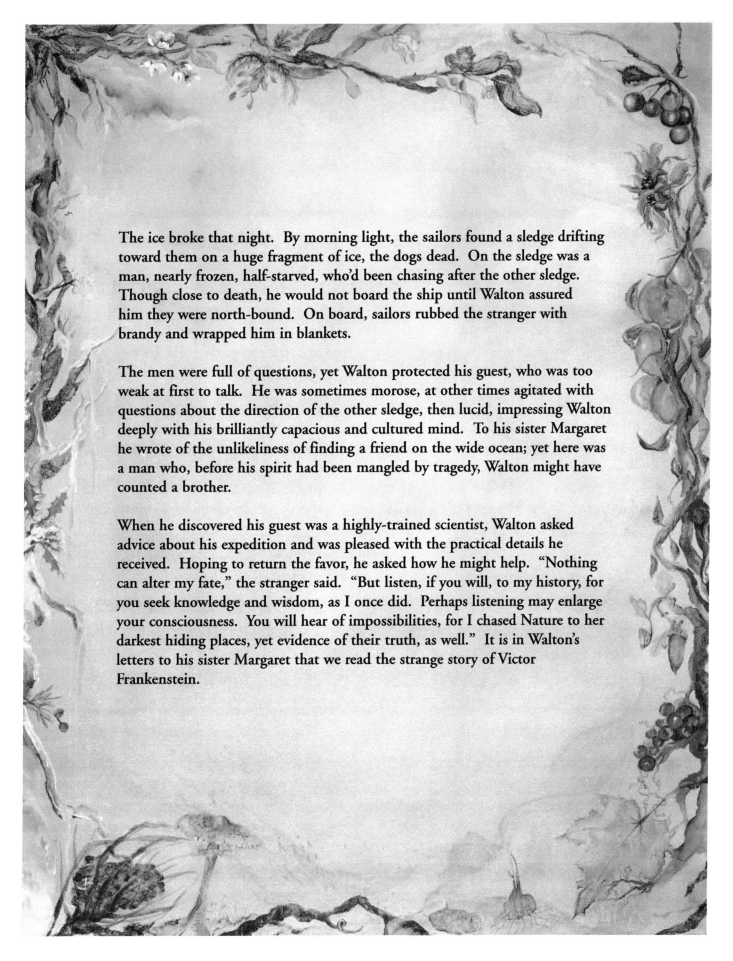

The ice broke that night. By morning light, the sailors found a sledge drifting toward them on a huge fragment of ice, the dogs dead. On the sledge was a man, nearly frozen, half-starved, who'd been chasing after the other sledge. Though close to death, he would not board the ship until Walton assured him they were north-bound. On board, sailors rubbed the stranger with brandy and wrapped him in blankets.

The men were full of questions, yet Walton protected his guest, who was too weak at first to talk. He was sometimes morose, at other times agitated with questions about the direction of the other sledge, then lucid, impressing Walton deeply with his brilliantly capacious and cultured mind. To his sister Margaret he wrote of the unlikeliness of finding a friend on the wide ocean; yet here was a man who, before his spirit had been mangled by tragedy, Walton might have counted a brother.

When he discovered his guest was a highly-trained scientist, Walton asked advice about his expedition and was pleased with the practical details he received. Hoping to return the favor, he asked how he might help. "Nothing can alter my fate," the stranger said. "But listen, if you will, to my history, for you seek knowledge and wisdom, as I once did. Perhaps listening may enlarge your consciousness. You will hear of impossibilities, for I chased Nature to her darkest hiding places, yet evidence of their truth, as well." It is in Walton's letters to his sister Margaret that we read the strange story of Victor Frankenstein.

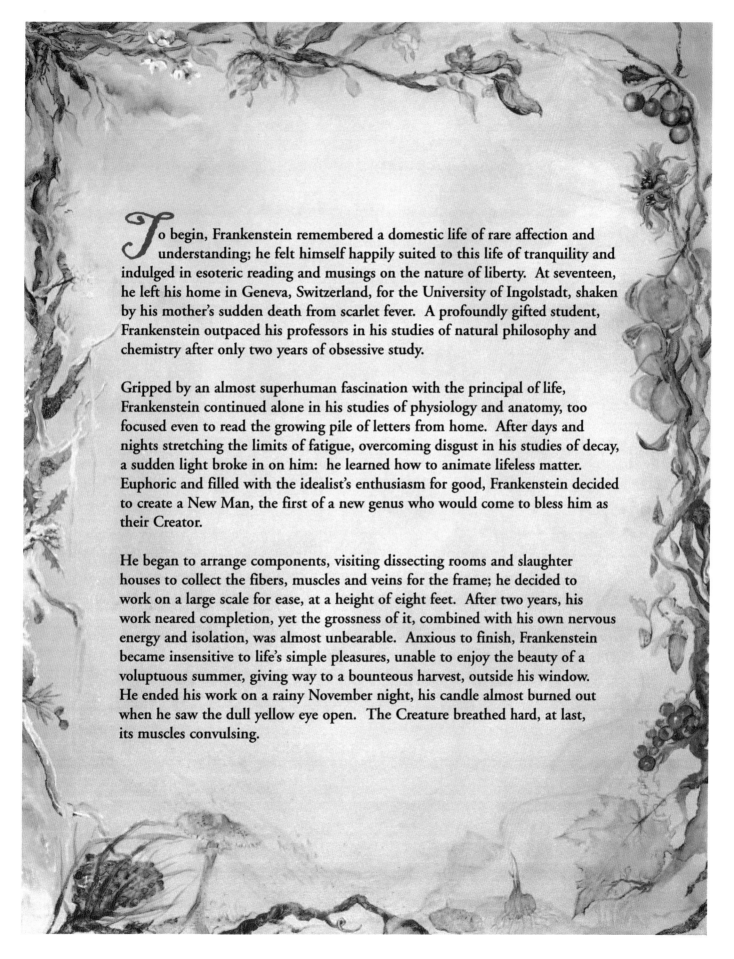

To begin, Frankenstein remembered a domestic life of rare affection and understanding; he felt himself happily suited to this life of tranquility and indulged in esoteric reading and musings on the nature of liberty. At seventeen, he left his home in Geneva, Switzerland, for the University of Ingolstadt, shaken by his mother's sudden death from scarlet fever. A profoundly gifted student, Frankenstein outpaced his professors in his studies of natural philosophy and chemistry after only two years of obsessive study.

Gripped by an almost superhuman fascination with the principal of life, Frankenstein continued alone in his studies of physiology and anatomy, too focused even to read the growing pile of letters from home. After days and nights stretching the limits of fatigue, overcoming disgust in his studies of decay, a sudden light broke in on him: he learned how to animate lifeless matter. Euphoric and filled with the idealist's enthusiasm for good, Frankenstein decided to create a New Man, the first of a new genus who would come to bless him as their Creator.

He began to arrange components, visiting dissecting rooms and slaughter houses to collect the fibers, muscles and veins for the frame; he decided to work on a large scale for ease, at a height of eight feet. After two years, his work neared completion, yet the grossness of it, combined with his own nervous energy and isolation, was almost unbearable. Anxious to finish, Frankenstein became insensitive to life's simple pleasures, unable to enjoy the beauty of a voluptuous summer, giving way to a bounteous harvest, outside his window. He ended his work on a rainy November night, his candle almost burned out when he saw the dull yellow eye open. The Creature breathed hard, at last, its muscles convulsing.

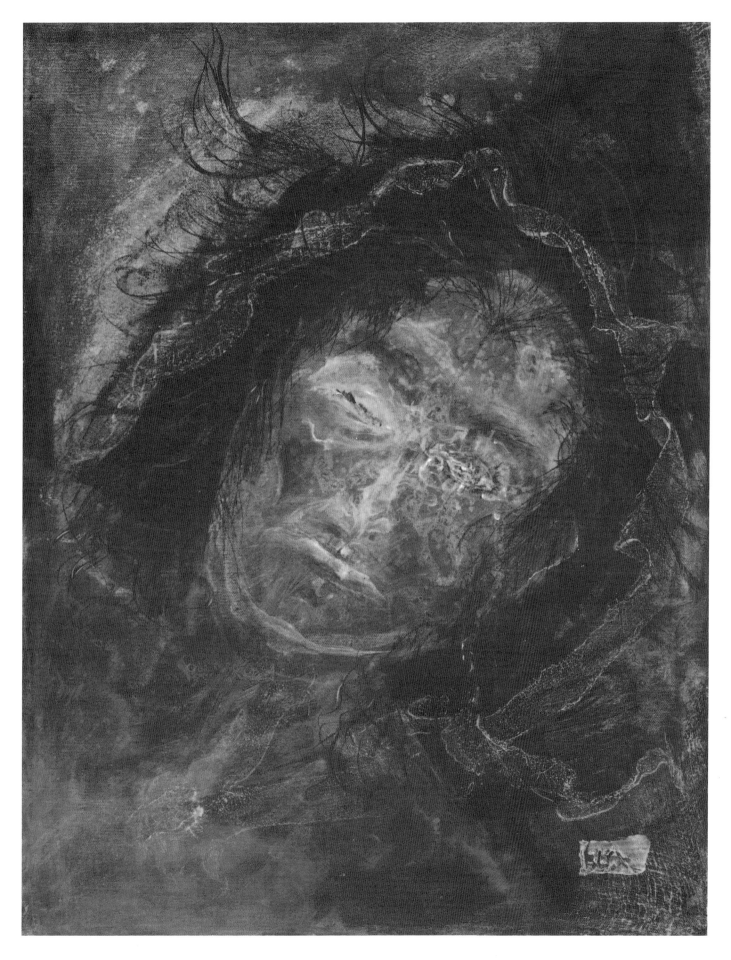

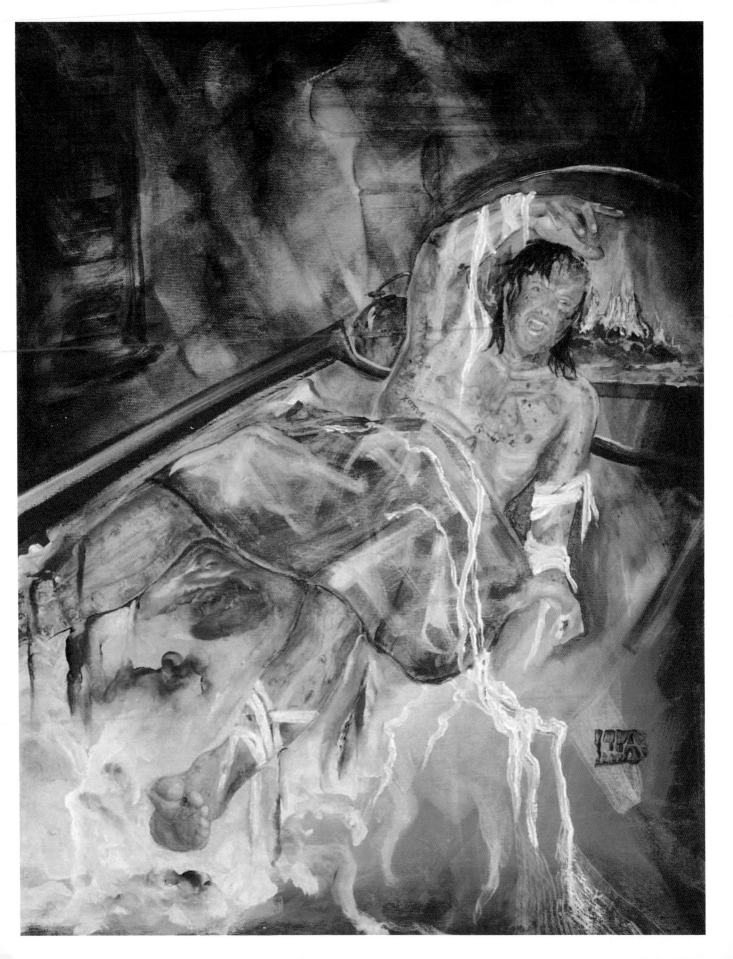

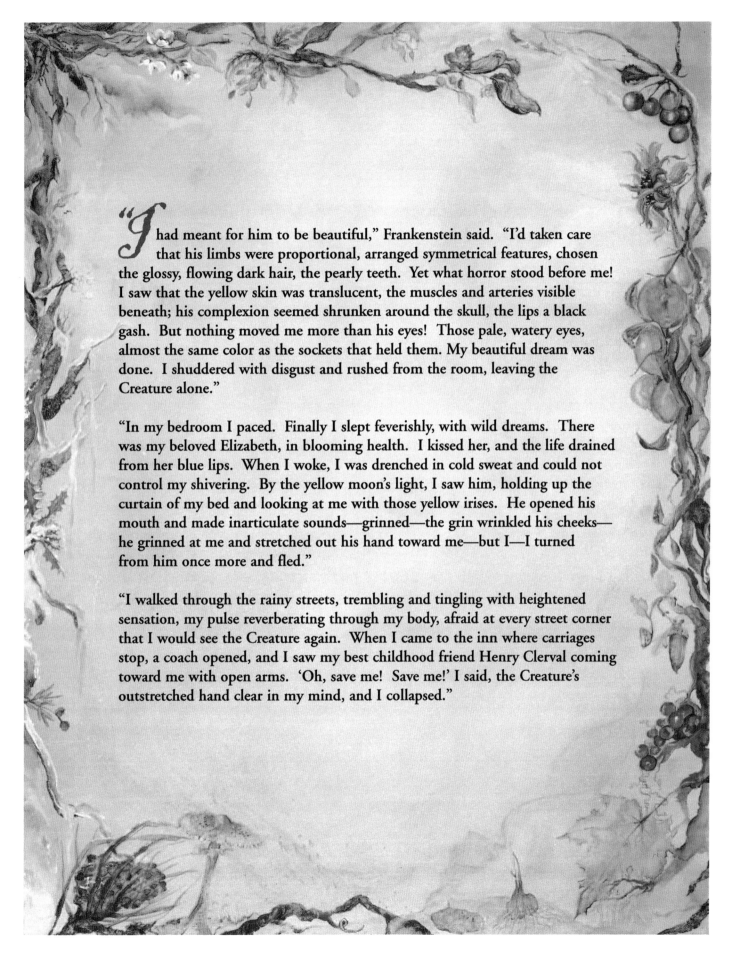

"I had meant for him to be beautiful," Frankenstein said. "I'd taken care that his limbs were proportional, arranged symmetrical features, chosen the glossy, flowing dark hair, the pearly teeth. Yet what horror stood before me! I saw that the yellow skin was translucent, the muscles and arteries visible beneath; his complexion seemed shrunken around the skull, the lips a black gash. But nothing moved me more than his eyes! Those pale, watery eyes, almost the same color as the sockets that held them. My beautiful dream was done. I shuddered with disgust and rushed from the room, leaving the Creature alone."

"In my bedroom I paced. Finally I slept feverishly, with wild dreams. There was my beloved Elizabeth, in blooming health. I kissed her, and the life drained from her blue lips. When I woke, I was drenched in cold sweat and could not control my shivering. By the yellow moon's light, I saw him, holding up the curtain of my bed and looking at me with those yellow irises. He opened his mouth and made inarticulate sounds—grinned—the grin wrinkled his cheeks—he grinned at me and stretched out his hand toward me—but I—I turned from him once more and fled."

"I walked through the rainy streets, trembling and tingling with heightened sensation, my pulse reverberating through my body, afraid at every street corner that I would see the Creature again. When I came to the inn where carriages stop, a coach opened, and I saw my best childhood friend Henry Clerval coming toward me with open arms. 'Oh, save me! Save me!' I said, the Creature's outstretched hand clear in my mind, and I collapsed."

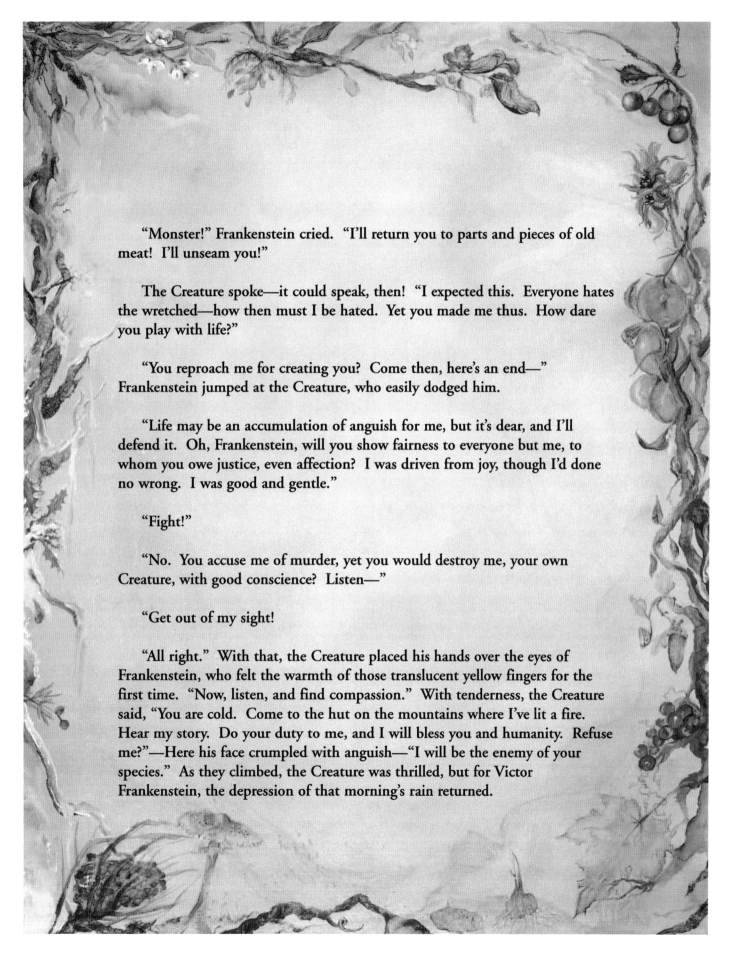

"Monster!" Frankenstein cried. "I'll return you to parts and pieces of old meat! I'll unseam you!"

The Creature spoke—it could speak, then! "I expected this. Everyone hates the wretched—how then must I be hated. Yet you made me thus. How dare you play with life?"

"You reproach me for creating you? Come then, here's an end—" Frankenstein jumped at the Creature, who easily dodged him.

"Life may be an accumulation of anguish for me, but it's dear, and I'll defend it. Oh, Frankenstein, will you show fairness to everyone but me, to whom you owe justice, even affection? I was driven from joy, though I'd done no wrong. I was good and gentle."

"Fight!"

"No. You accuse me of murder, yet you would destroy me, your own Creature, with good conscience? Listen—"

"Get out of my sight!

"All right." With that, the Creature placed his hands over the eyes of Frankenstein, who felt the warmth of those translucent yellow fingers for the first time. "Now, listen, and find compassion." With tenderness, the Creature said, "You are cold. Come to the hut on the mountains where I've lit a fire. Hear my story. Do your duty to me, and I will bless you and humanity. Refuse me?"—Here his face crumpled with anguish—"I will be the enemy of your species." As they climbed, the Creature was thrilled, but for Victor Frankenstein, the depression of that morning's rain returned.

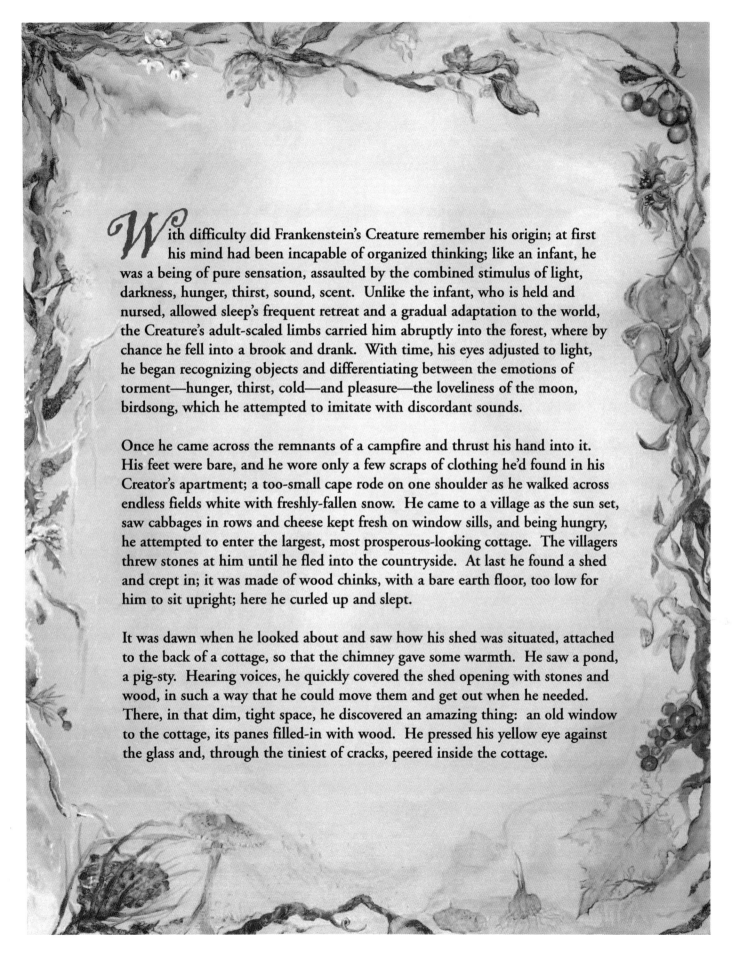

With difficulty did Frankenstein's Creature remember his origin; at first his mind had been incapable of organized thinking; like an infant, he was a being of pure sensation, assaulted by the combined stimulus of light, darkness, hunger, thirst, sound, scent. Unlike the infant, who is held and nursed, allowed sleep's frequent retreat and a gradual adaptation to the world, the Creature's adult-scaled limbs carried him abruptly into the forest, where by chance he fell into a brook and drank. With time, his eyes adjusted to light, he began recognizing objects and differentiating between the emotions of torment—hunger, thirst, cold—and pleasure—the loveliness of the moon, birdsong, which he attempted to imitate with discordant sounds.

Once he came across the remnants of a campfire and thrust his hand into it. His feet were bare, and he wore only a few scraps of clothing he'd found in his Creator's apartment; a too-small cape rode on one shoulder as he walked across endless fields white with freshly-fallen snow. He came to a village as the sun set, saw cabbages in rows and cheese kept fresh on window sills, and being hungry, he attempted to enter the largest, most prosperous-looking cottage. The villagers threw stones at him until he fled into the countryside. At last he found a shed and crept in; it was made of wood chinks, with a bare earth floor, too low for him to sit upright; here he curled up and slept.

It was dawn when he looked about and saw how his shed was situated, attached to the back of a cottage, so that the chimney gave some warmth. He saw a pond, a pig-sty. Hearing voices, he quickly covered the shed opening with stones and wood, in such a way that he could move them and get out when he needed. There, in that dim, tight space, he discovered an amazing thing: an old window to the cottage, its panes filled-in with wood. He pressed his yellow eye against the glass and, through the tiniest of cracks, peered inside the cottage.

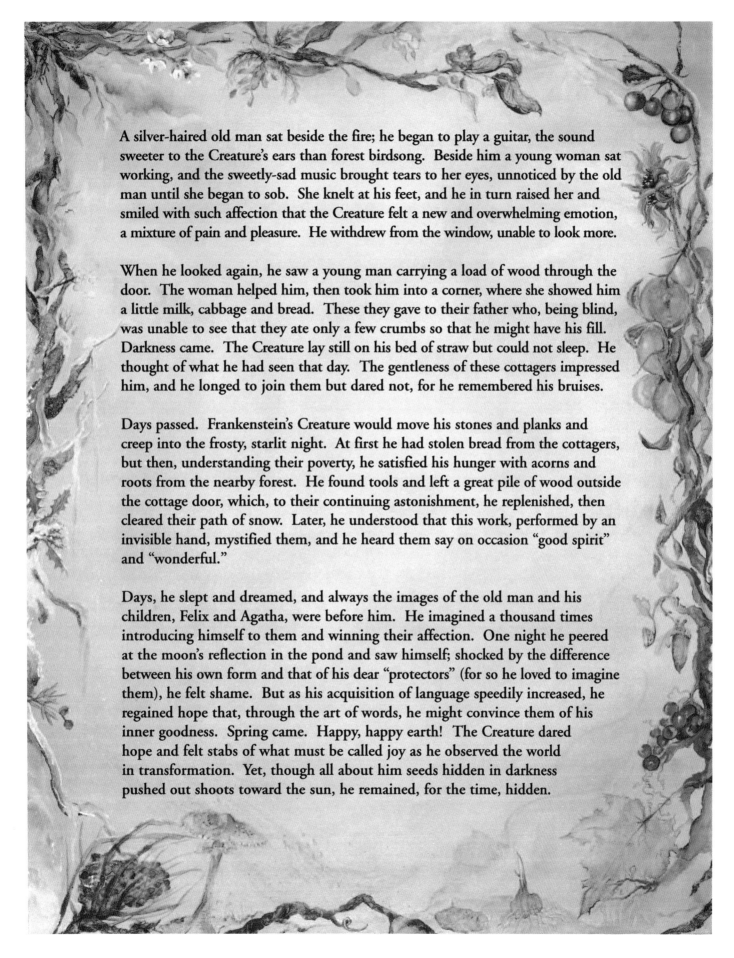

A silver-haired old man sat beside the fire; he began to play a guitar, the sound sweeter to the Creature's ears than forest birdsong. Beside him a young woman sat working, and the sweetly-sad music brought tears to her eyes, unnoticed by the old man until she began to sob. She knelt at his feet, and he in turn raised her and smiled with such affection that the Creature felt a new and overwhelming emotion, a mixture of pain and pleasure. He withdrew from the window, unable to look more.

When he looked again, he saw a young man carrying a load of wood through the door. The woman helped him, then took him into a corner, where she showed him a little milk, cabbage and bread. These they gave to their father who, being blind, was unable to see that they ate only a few crumbs so that he might have his fill. Darkness came. The Creature lay still on his bed of straw but could not sleep. He thought of what he had seen that day. The gentleness of these cottagers impressed him, and he longed to join them but dared not, for he remembered his bruises.

Days passed. Frankenstein's Creature would move his stones and planks and creep into the frosty, starlit night. At first he had stolen bread from the cottagers, but then, understanding their poverty, he satisfied his hunger with acorns and roots from the nearby forest. He found tools and left a great pile of wood outside the cottage door, which, to their continuing astonishment, he replenished, then cleared their path of snow. Later, he understood that this work, performed by an invisible hand, mystified them, and he heard them say on occasion "good spirit" and "wonderful."

Days, he slept and dreamed, and always the images of the old man and his children, Felix and Agatha, were before him. He imagined a thousand times introducing himself to them and winning their affection. One night he peered at the moon's reflection in the pond and saw himself; shocked by the difference between his own form and that of his dear "protectors" (for so he loved to imagine them), he felt shame. But as his acquisition of language speedily increased, he regained hope that, through the art of words, he might convince them of his inner goodness. Spring came. Happy, happy earth! The Creature dared hope and felt stabs of what must be called joy as he observed the world in transformation. Yet, though all about him seeds hidden in darkness pushed out shoots toward the sun, he remained, for the time, hidden.

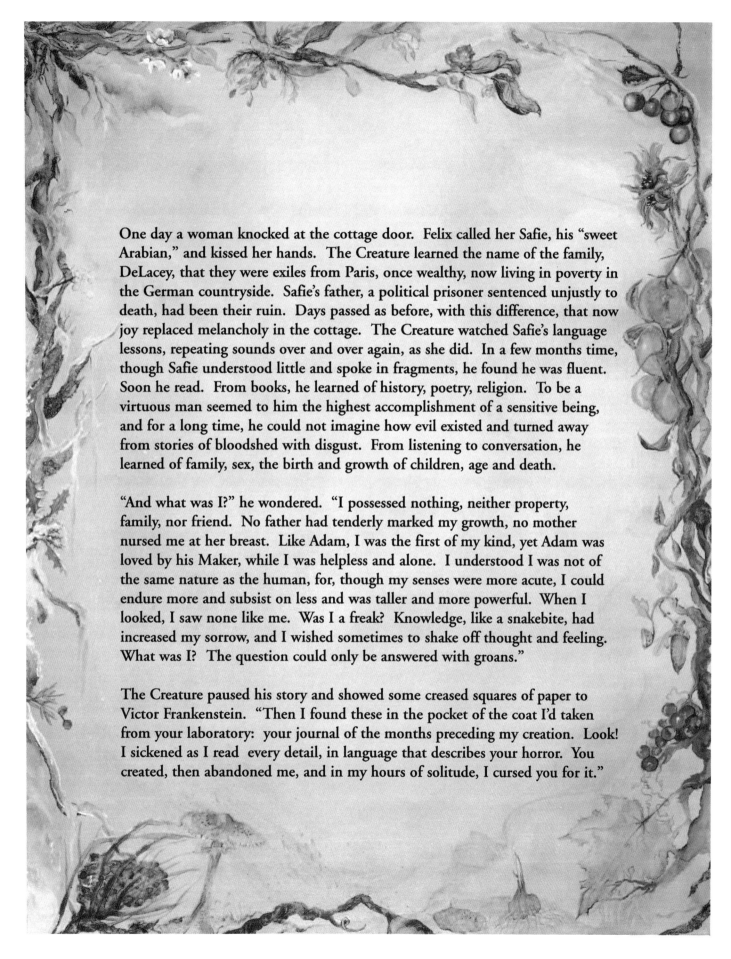

One day a woman knocked at the cottage door. Felix called her Safie, his "sweet Arabian," and kissed her hands. The Creature learned the name of the family, DeLacey, that they were exiles from Paris, once wealthy, now living in poverty in the German countryside. Safie's father, a political prisoner sentenced unjustly to death, had been their ruin. Days passed as before, with this difference, that now joy replaced melancholy in the cottage. The Creature watched Safie's language lessons, repeating sounds over and over again, as she did. In a few months time, though Safie understood little and spoke in fragments, he found he was fluent. Soon he read. From books, he learned of history, poetry, religion. To be a virtuous man seemed to him the highest accomplishment of a sensitive being, and for a long time, he could not imagine how evil existed and turned away from stories of bloodshed with disgust. From listening to conversation, he learned of family, sex, the birth and growth of children, age and death.

"And what was I?" he wondered. "I possessed nothing, neither property, family, nor friend. No father had tenderly marked my growth, no mother nursed me at her breast. Like Adam, I was the first of my kind, yet Adam was loved by his Maker, while I was helpless and alone. I understood I was not of the same nature as the human, for, though my senses were more acute, I could endure more and subsist on less and was taller and more powerful. When I looked, I saw none like me. Was I a freak? Knowledge, like a snakebite, had increased my sorrow, and I wished sometimes to shake off thought and feeling. What was I? The question could only be answered with groans."

The Creature paused his story and showed some creased squares of paper to Victor Frankenstein. "Then I found these in the pocket of the coat I'd taken from your laboratory: your journal of the months preceding my creation. Look! I sickened as I read every detail, in language that describes your horror. You created, then abandoned me, and in my hours of solitude, I cursed you for it."

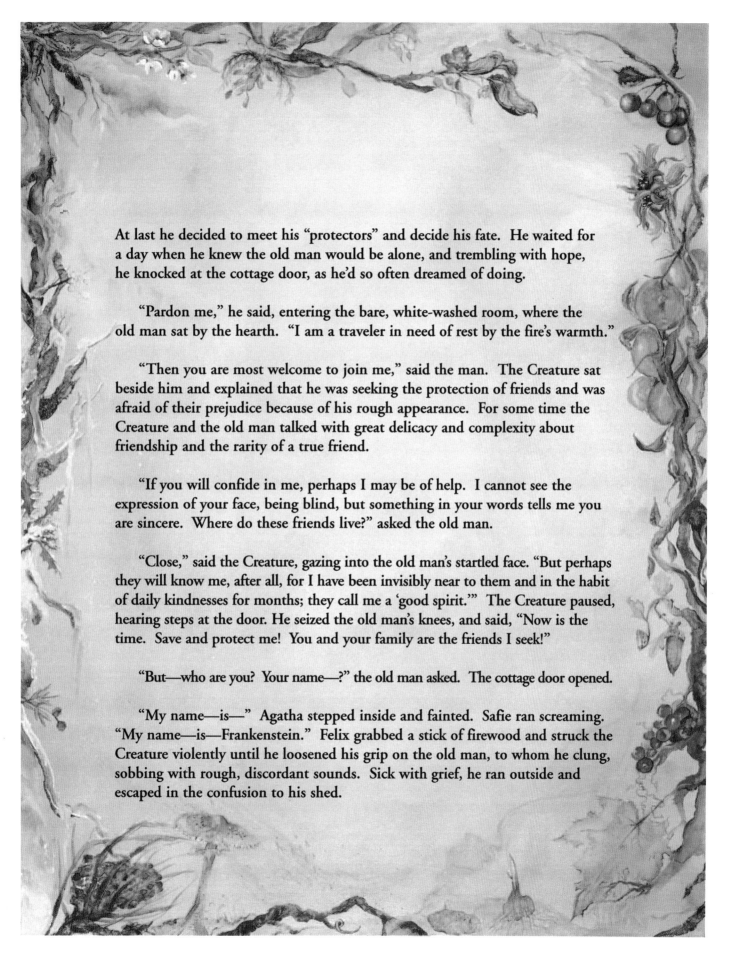

At last he decided to meet his "protectors" and decide his fate. He waited for a day when he knew the old man would be alone, and trembling with hope, he knocked at the cottage door, as he'd so often dreamed of doing.

"Pardon me," he said, entering the bare, white-washed room, where the old man sat by the hearth. "I am a traveler in need of rest by the fire's warmth."

"Then you are most welcome to join me," said the man. The Creature sat beside him and explained that he was seeking the protection of friends and was afraid of their prejudice because of his rough appearance. For some time the Creature and the old man talked with great delicacy and complexity about friendship and the rarity of a true friend.

"If you will confide in me, perhaps I may be of help. I cannot see the expression of your face, being blind, but something in your words tells me you are sincere. Where do these friends live?" asked the old man.

"Close," said the Creature, gazing into the old man's startled face. "But perhaps they will know me, after all, for I have been invisibly near to them and in the habit of daily kindnesses for months; they call me a 'good spirit.'" The Creature paused, hearing steps at the door. He seized the old man's knees, and said, "Now is the time. Save and protect me! You and your family are the friends I seek!"

"But—who are you? Your name—?" the old man asked. The cottage door opened.

"My name—is—" Agatha stepped inside and fainted. Safie ran screaming. "My name—is—Frankenstein." Felix grabbed a stick of firewood and struck the Creature violently until he loosened his grip on the old man, to whom he clung, sobbing with rough, discordant sounds. Sick with grief, he ran outside and escaped in the confusion to his shed.

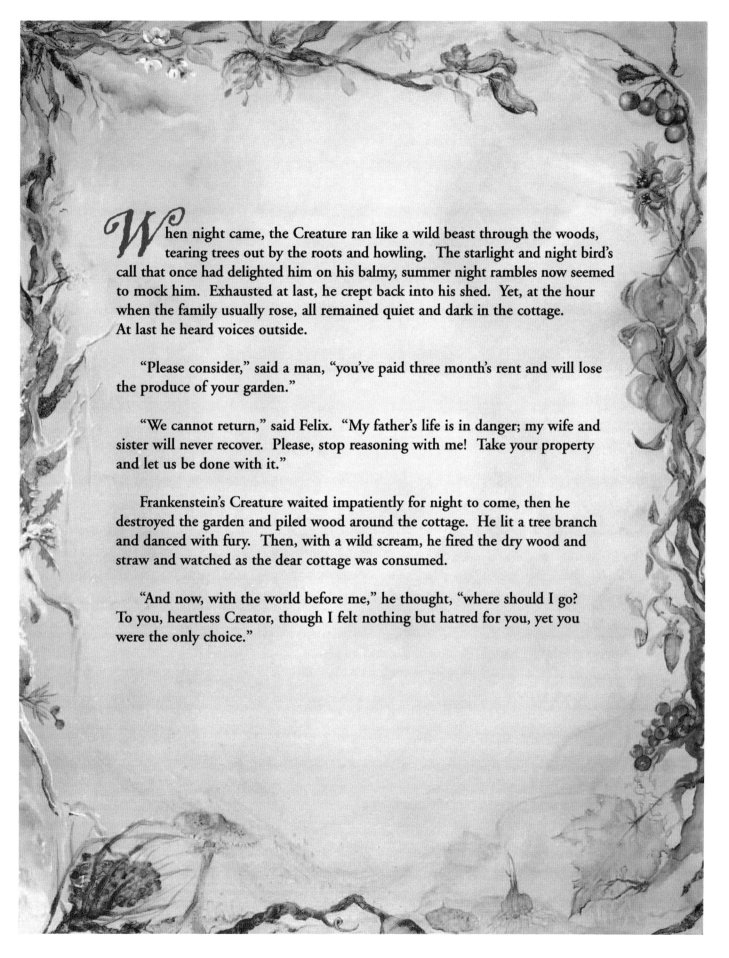

When night came, the Creature ran like a wild beast through the woods, tearing trees out by the roots and howling. The starlight and night bird's call that once had delighted him on his balmy, summer night rambles now seemed to mock him. Exhausted at last, he crept back into his shed. Yet, at the hour when the family usually rose, all remained quiet and dark in the cottage. At last he heard voices outside.

"Please consider," said a man, "you've paid three month's rent and will lose the produce of your garden."

"We cannot return," said Felix. "My father's life is in danger; my wife and sister will never recover. Please, stop reasoning with me! Take your property and let us be done with it."

Frankenstein's Creature waited impatiently for night to come, then he destroyed the garden and piled wood around the cottage. He lit a tree branch and danced with fury. Then, with a wild scream, he fired the dry wood and straw and watched as the dear cottage was consumed.

"And now, with the world before me," he thought, "where should I go? To you, heartless Creator, though I felt nothing but hatred for you, yet you were the only choice."

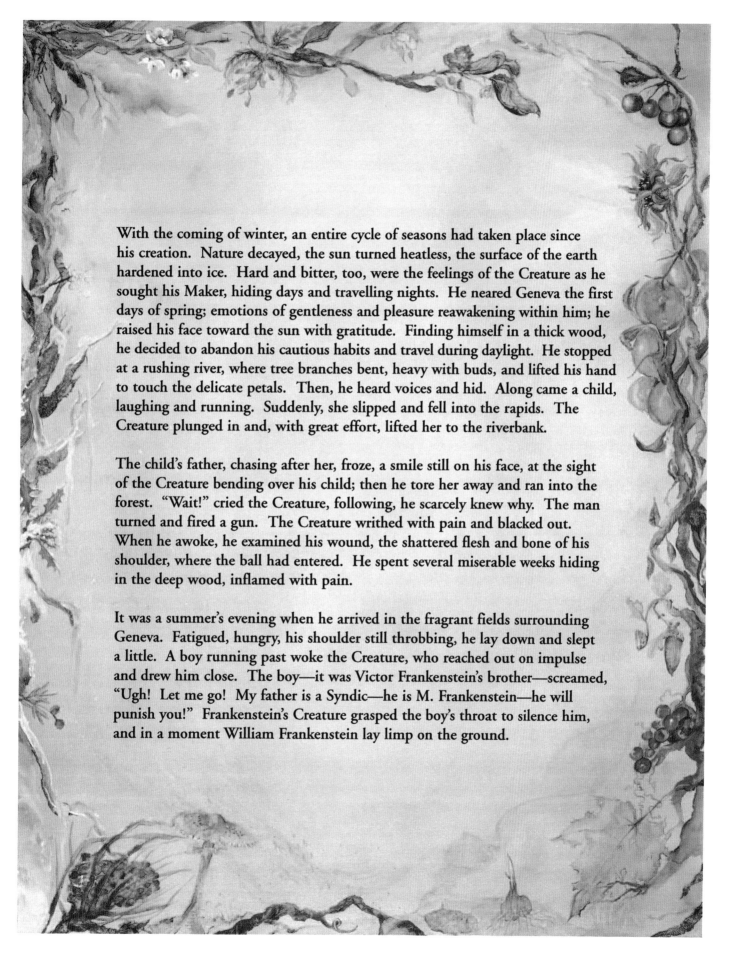

With the coming of winter, an entire cycle of seasons had taken place since his creation. Nature decayed, the sun turned heatless, the surface of the earth hardened into ice. Hard and bitter, too, were the feelings of the Creature as he sought his Maker, hiding days and travelling nights. He neared Geneva the first days of spring; emotions of gentleness and pleasure reawakening within him; he raised his face toward the sun with gratitude. Finding himself in a thick wood, he decided to abandon his cautious habits and travel during daylight. He stopped at a rushing river, where tree branches bent, heavy with buds, and lifted his hand to touch the delicate petals. Then, he heard voices and hid. Along came a child, laughing and running. Suddenly, she slipped and fell into the rapids. The Creature plunged in and, with great effort, lifted her to the riverbank.

The child's father, chasing after her, froze, a smile still on his face, at the sight of the Creature bending over his child; then he tore her away and ran into the forest. "Wait!" cried the Creature, following, he scarcely knew why. The man turned and fired a gun. The Creature writhed with pain and blacked out. When he awoke, he examined his wound, the shattered flesh and bone of his shoulder, where the ball had entered. He spent several miserable weeks hiding in the deep wood, inflamed with pain.

It was a summer's evening when he arrived in the fragrant fields surrounding Geneva. Fatigued, hungry, his shoulder still throbbing, he lay down and slept a little. A boy running past woke the Creature, who reached out on impulse and drew him close. The boy—it was Victor Frankenstein's brother—screamed, "Ugh! Let me go! My father is a Syndic—he is M. Frankenstein—he will punish you!" Frankenstein's Creature grasped the boy's throat to silence him, and in a moment William Frankenstein lay limp on the ground.

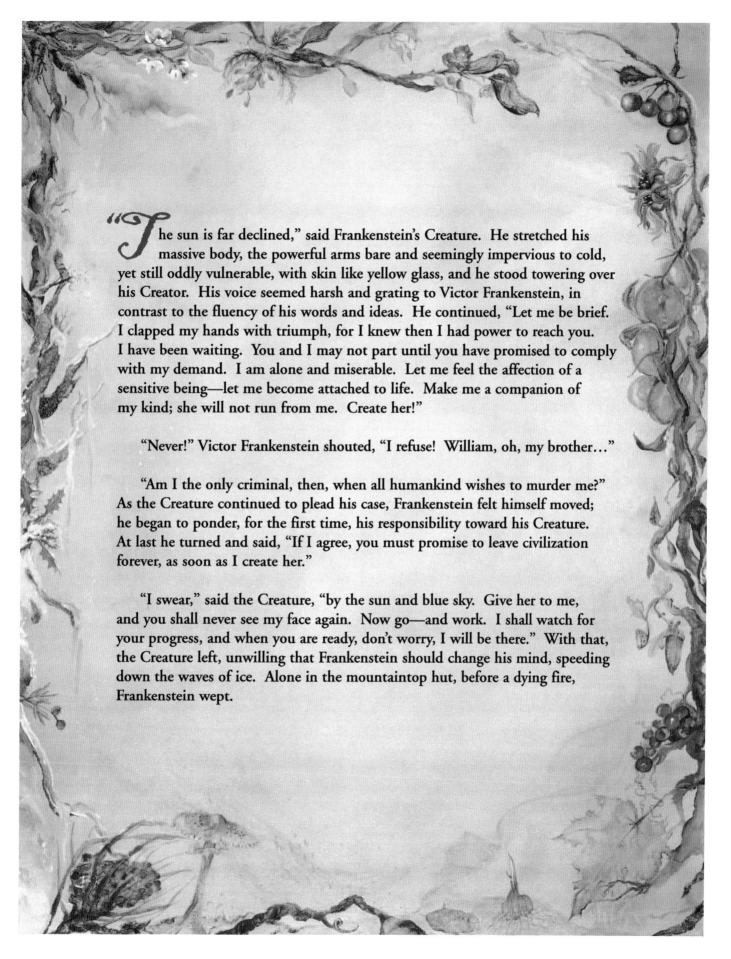

"The sun is far declined," said Frankenstein's Creature. He stretched his massive body, the powerful arms bare and seemingly impervious to cold, yet still oddly vulnerable, with skin like yellow glass, and he stood towering over his Creator. His voice seemed harsh and grating to Victor Frankenstein, in contrast to the fluency of his words and ideas. He continued, "Let me be brief. I clapped my hands with triumph, for I knew then I had power to reach you. I have been waiting. You and I may not part until you have promised to comply with my demand. I am alone and miserable. Let me feel the affection of a sensitive being—let me become attached to life. Make me a companion of my kind; she will not run from me. Create her!"

"Never!" Victor Frankenstein shouted, "I refuse! William, oh, my brother…"

"Am I the only criminal, then, when all humankind wishes to murder me?" As the Creature continued to plead his case, Frankenstein felt himself moved; he began to ponder, for the first time, his responsibility toward his Creature. At last he turned and said, "If I agree, you must promise to leave civilization forever, as soon as I create her."

"I swear," said the Creature, "by the sun and blue sky. Give her to me, and you shall never see my face again. Now go—and work. I shall watch for your progress, and when you are ready, don't worry, I will be there." With that, the Creature left, unwilling that Frankenstein should change his mind, speeding down the waves of ice. Alone in the mountaintop hut, before a dying fire, Frankenstein wept.

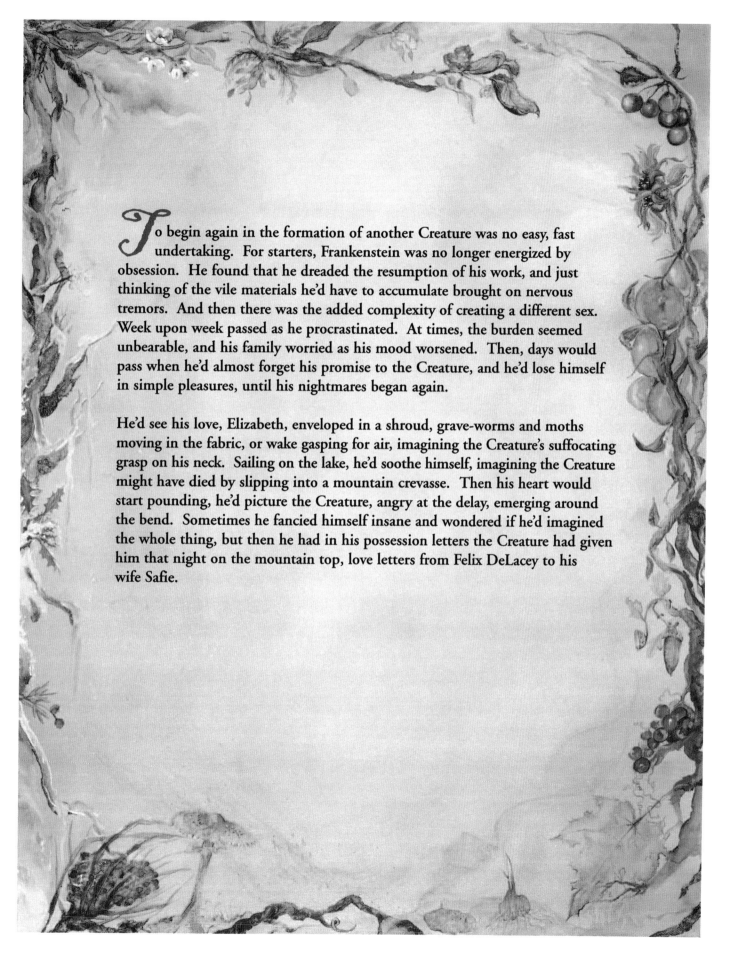

To begin again in the formation of another Creature was no easy, fast undertaking. For starters, Frankenstein was no longer energized by obsession. He found that he dreaded the resumption of his work, and just thinking of the vile materials he'd have to accumulate brought on nervous tremors. And then there was the added complexity of creating a different sex. Week upon week passed as he procrastinated. At times, the burden seemed unbearable, and his family worried as his mood worsened. Then, days would pass when he'd almost forget his promise to the Creature, and he'd lose himself in simple pleasures, until his nightmares began again.

He'd see his love, Elizabeth, enveloped in a shroud, grave-worms and moths moving in the fabric, or wake gasping for air, imagining the Creature's suffocating grasp on his neck. Sailing on the lake, he'd soothe himself, imagining the Creature might have died by slipping into a mountain crevasse. Then his heart would start pounding, he'd picture the Creature, angry at the delay, emerging around the bend. Sometimes he fancied himself insane and wondered if he'd imagined the whole thing, but then he had in his possession letters the Creature had given him that night on the mountain top, love letters from Felix DeLacey to his wife Safie.

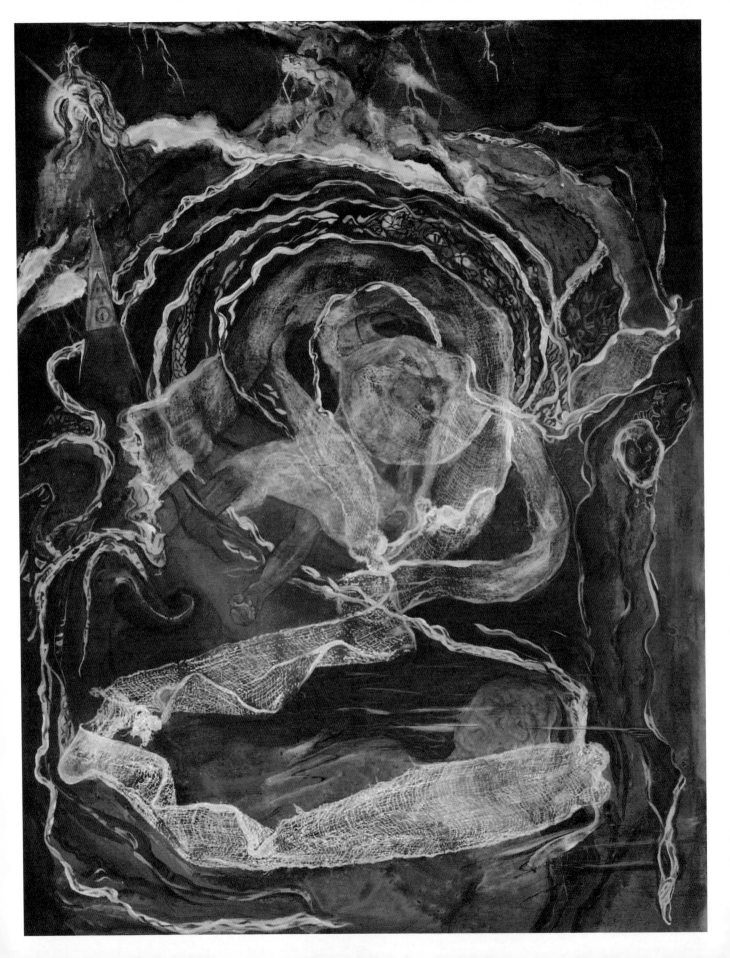

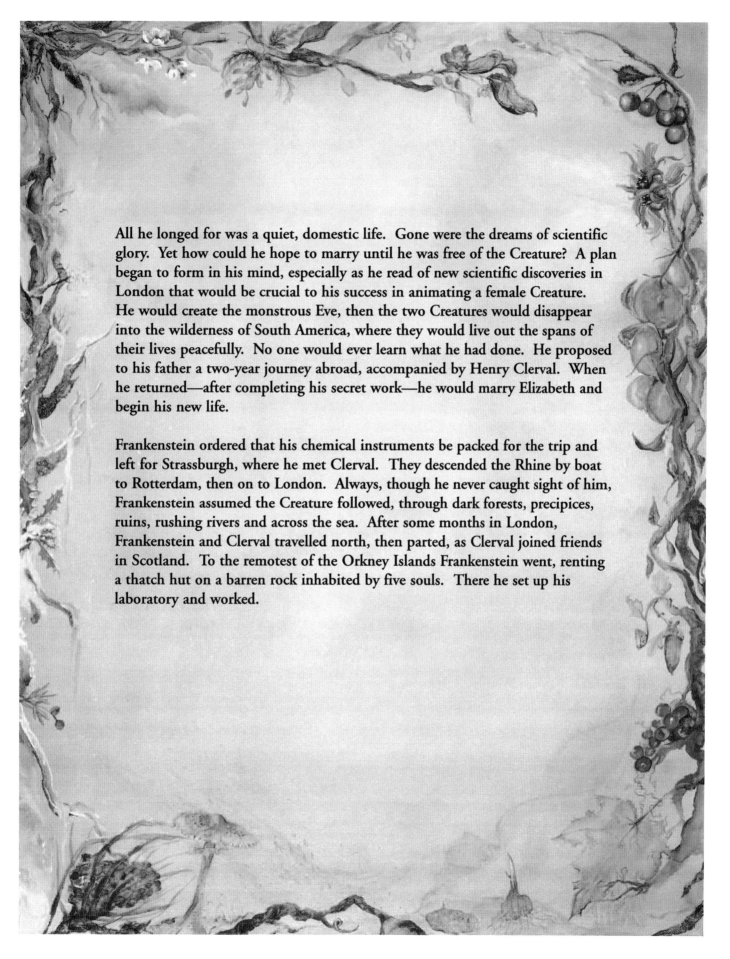

All he longed for was a quiet, domestic life. Gone were the dreams of scientific glory. Yet how could he hope to marry until he was free of the Creature? A plan began to form in his mind, especially as he read of new scientific discoveries in London that would be crucial to his success in animating a female Creature. He would create the monstrous Eve, then the two Creatures would disappear into the wilderness of South America, where they would live out the spans of their lives peacefully. No one would ever learn what he had done. He proposed to his father a two-year journey abroad, accompanied by Henry Clerval. When he returned—after completing his secret work—he would marry Elizabeth and begin his new life.

Frankenstein ordered that his chemical instruments be packed for the trip and left for Strassburgh, where he met Clerval. They descended the Rhine by boat to Rotterdam, then on to London. Always, though he never caught sight of him, Frankenstein assumed the Creature followed, through dark forests, precipices, ruins, rushing rivers and across the sea. After some months in London, Frankenstein and Clerval travelled north, then parted, as Clerval joined friends in Scotland. To the remotest of the Orkney Islands Frankenstein went, renting a thatch hut on a barren rock inhabited by five souls. There he set up his laboratory and worked.

"No Eve soothed my sorrows...

"Or shared my thoughts; I was alone."

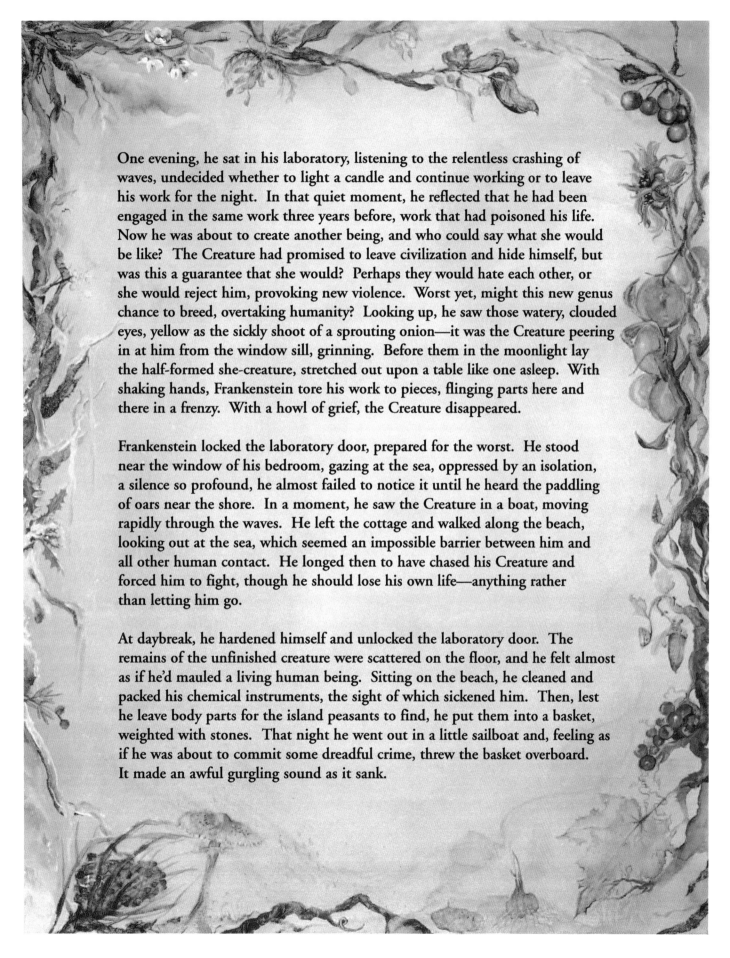

One evening, he sat in his laboratory, listening to the relentless crashing of waves, undecided whether to light a candle and continue working or to leave his work for the night. In that quiet moment, he reflected that he had been engaged in the same work three years before, work that had poisoned his life. Now he was about to create another being, and who could say what she would be like? The Creature had promised to leave civilization and hide himself, but was this a guarantee that she would? Perhaps they would hate each other, or she would reject him, provoking new violence. Worst yet, might this new genus chance to breed, overtaking humanity? Looking up, he saw those watery, clouded eyes, yellow as the sickly shoot of a sprouting onion—it was the Creature peering in at him from the window sill, grinning. Before them in the moonlight lay the half-formed she-creature, stretched out upon a table like one asleep. With shaking hands, Frankenstein tore his work to pieces, flinging parts here and there in a frenzy. With a howl of grief, the Creature disappeared.

Frankenstein locked the laboratory door, prepared for the worst. He stood near the window of his bedroom, gazing at the sea, oppressed by an isolation, a silence so profound, he almost failed to notice it until he heard the paddling of oars near the shore. In a moment, he saw the Creature in a boat, moving rapidly through the waves. He left the cottage and walked along the beach, looking out at the sea, which seemed an impossible barrier between him and all other human contact. He longed then to have chased his Creature and forced him to fight, though he should lose his own life—anything rather than letting him go.

At daybreak, he hardened himself and unlocked the laboratory door. The remains of the unfinished creature were scattered on the floor, and he felt almost as if he'd mauled a living human being. Sitting on the beach, he cleaned and packed his chemical instruments, the sight of which sickened him. Then, lest he leave body parts for the island peasants to find, he put them into a basket, weighted with stones. That night he went out in a little sailboat and, feeling as if he was about to commit some dreadful crime, threw the basket overboard. It made an awful gurgling sound as it sank.

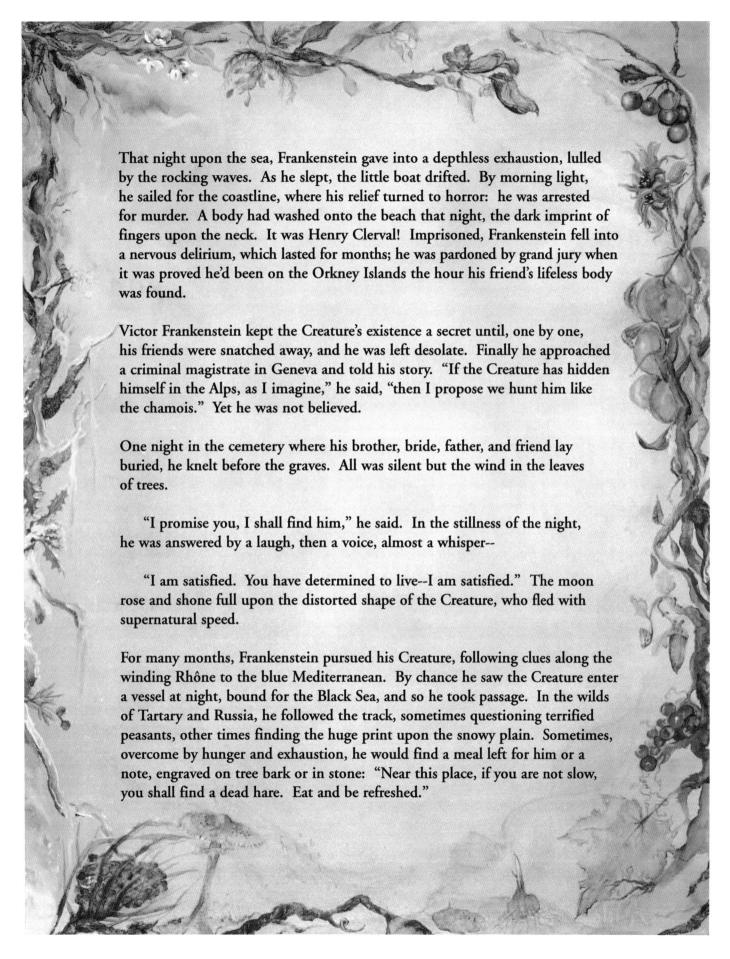

That night upon the sea, Frankenstein gave into a depthless exhaustion, lulled by the rocking waves. As he slept, the little boat drifted. By morning light, he sailed for the coastline, where his relief turned to horror: he was arrested for murder. A body had washed onto the beach that night, the dark imprint of fingers upon the neck. It was Henry Clerval! Imprisoned, Frankenstein fell into a nervous delirium, which lasted for months; he was pardoned by grand jury when it was proved he'd been on the Orkney Islands the hour his friend's lifeless body was found.

Victor Frankenstein kept the Creature's existence a secret until, one by one, his friends were snatched away, and he was left desolate. Finally he approached a criminal magistrate in Geneva and told his story. "If the Creature has hidden himself in the Alps, as I imagine," he said, "then I propose we hunt him like the chamois." Yet he was not believed.

One night in the cemetery where his brother, bride, father, and friend lay buried, he knelt before the graves. All was silent but the wind in the leaves of trees.

"I promise you, I shall find him," he said. In the stillness of the night, he was answered by a laugh, then a voice, almost a whisper--

"I am satisfied. You have determined to live--I am satisfied." The moon rose and shone full upon the distorted shape of the Creature, who fled with supernatural speed.

For many months, Frankenstein pursued his Creature, following clues along the winding Rhône to the blue Mediterranean. By chance he saw the Creature enter a vessel at night, bound for the Black Sea, and so he took passage. In the wilds of Tartary and Russia, he followed the track, sometimes questioning terrified peasants, other times finding the huge print upon the snowy plain. Sometimes, overcome by hunger and exhaustion, he would find a meal left for him or a note, engraved on tree bark or in stone: "Near this place, if you are not slow, you shall find a dead hare. Eat and be refreshed."

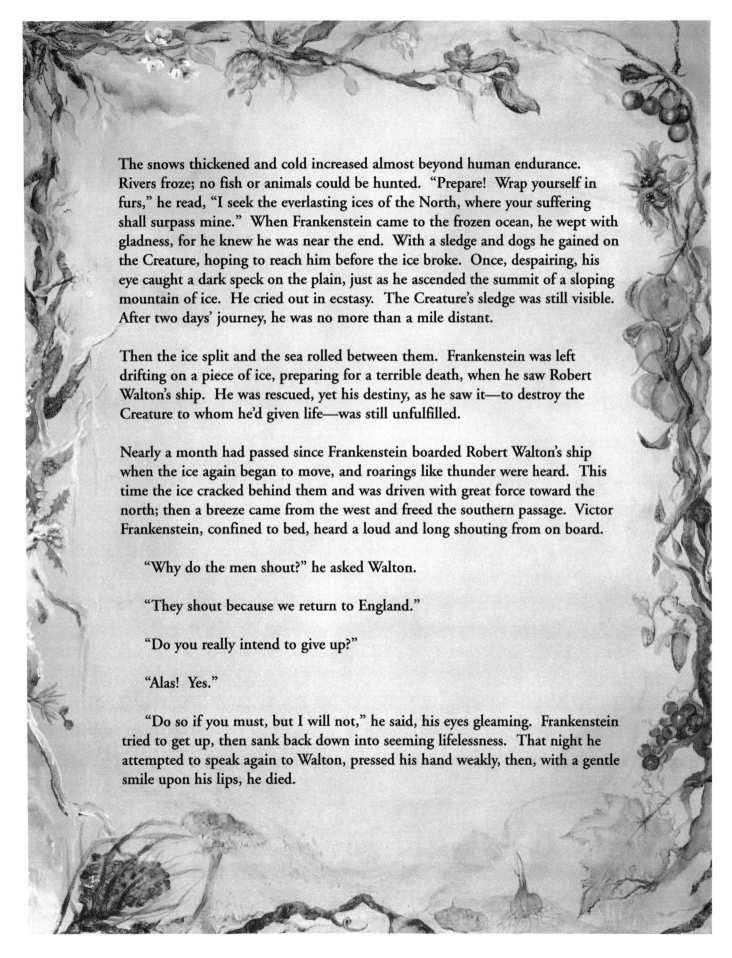

The snows thickened and cold increased almost beyond human endurance. Rivers froze; no fish or animals could be hunted. "Prepare! Wrap yourself in furs," he read, "I seek the everlasting ices of the North, where your suffering shall surpass mine." When Frankenstein came to the frozen ocean, he wept with gladness, for he knew he was near the end. With a sledge and dogs he gained on the Creature, hoping to reach him before the ice broke. Once, despairing, his eye caught a dark speck on the plain, just as he ascended the summit of a sloping mountain of ice. He cried out in ecstasy. The Creature's sledge was still visible. After two days' journey, he was no more than a mile distant.

Then the ice split and the sea rolled between them. Frankenstein was left drifting on a piece of ice, preparing for a terrible death, when he saw Robert Walton's ship. He was rescued, yet his destiny, as he saw it—to destroy the Creature to whom he'd given life—was still unfulfilled.

Nearly a month had passed since Frankenstein boarded Robert Walton's ship when the ice again began to move, and roarings like thunder were heard. This time the ice cracked behind them and was driven with great force toward the north; then a breeze came from the west and freed the southern passage. Victor Frankenstein, confined to bed, heard a loud and long shouting from on board.

"Why do the men shout?" he asked Walton.

"They shout because we return to England."

"Do you really intend to give up?"

"Alas! Yes."

"Do so if you must, but I will not," he said, his eyes gleaming. Frankenstein tried to get up, then sank back down into seeming lifelessness. That night he attempted to speak again to Walton, pressed his hand weakly, then, with a gentle smile upon his lips, he died.

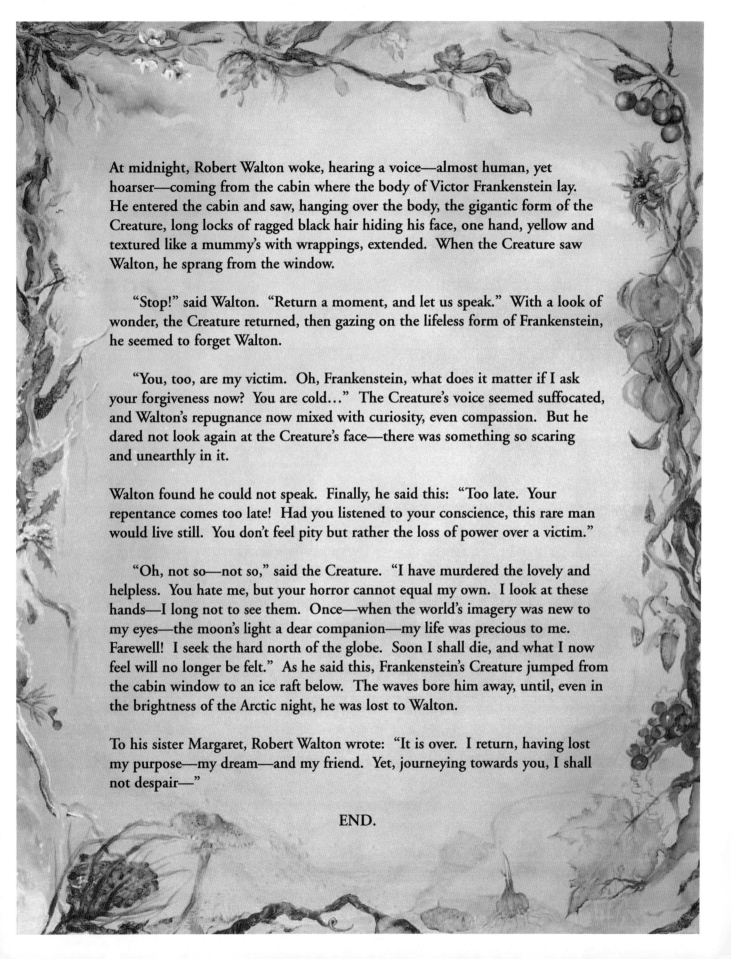

At midnight, Robert Walton woke, hearing a voice—almost human, yet hoarser—coming from the cabin where the body of Victor Frankenstein lay. He entered the cabin and saw, hanging over the body, the gigantic form of the Creature, long locks of ragged black hair hiding his face, one hand, yellow and textured like a mummy's with wrappings, extended. When the Creature saw Walton, he sprang from the window.

"Stop!" said Walton. "Return a moment, and let us speak." With a look of wonder, the Creature returned, then gazing on the lifeless form of Frankenstein, he seemed to forget Walton.

"You, too, are my victim. Oh, Frankenstein, what does it matter if I ask your forgiveness now? You are cold…" The Creature's voice seemed suffocated, and Walton's repugnance now mixed with curiosity, even compassion. But he dared not look again at the Creature's face—there was something so scaring and unearthly in it.

Walton found he could not speak. Finally, he said this: "Too late. Your repentance comes too late! Had you listened to your conscience, this rare man would live still. You don't feel pity but rather the loss of power over a victim."

"Oh, not so—not so," said the Creature. "I have murdered the lovely and helpless. You hate me, but your horror cannot equal my own. I look at these hands—I long not to see them. Once—when the world's imagery was new to my eyes—the moon's light a dear companion—my life was precious to me. Farewell! I seek the hard north of the globe. Soon I shall die, and what I now feel will no longer be felt." As he said this, Frankenstein's Creature jumped from the cabin window to an ice raft below. The waves bore him away, until, even in the brightness of the Arctic night, he was lost to Walton.

To his sister Margaret, Robert Walton wrote: "It is over. I return, having lost my purpose—my dream—and my friend. Yet, journeying towards you, I shall not despair—"

END.

Jennifer Anderson [signature]

Jennifer Anderson, a former Stegner Fellow in fiction writing at Stanford University, published her first story in *The Best American Mystery Stories 2001*, for which she later received a Pushcart honorable mention. The idea for this retelling began when her daughter, a precocious toddler, became uneasy reading a Halloween pop-up book with 'Lil' Frankie and 'Lil' Drac, and she realized her daughter needed a context to make sense of the characters. In re-familiarizing herself with Shelley's novel, she found sustenance for the difficult yet pleasurable work of mothering, nurturing the souls of children. She lives in Napa, California with her husband and two daughters, Pella and Sanna.

California artist Barbara Harris Anderson splits time between two studios, one on a ranch in Creston, California, the other in Sonoma. A self-taught and intuitive artist, she sought to convey both narrative action and emotional power in this series of paintings. The language of symbolism expands the visual experience into both scholarly and primal human dimensions, offering a story within a story. Experimenting with technique for the book's illustrations was a transformative experience; she drew upon common experiences of human suffering as she painted her son Kevin, the model for Victor Frankenstein. She writes, "I know my work is grounded precisely in the secret and sacred places of the mind and soul, an enthusiastic labor with a certain spirituality." This is her first picture book.

Made in the USA
Lexington, KY
20 October 2010